The Assistant

Josef Schabell

The Assistant

Radical Bookshop and Press
4838 Richard Road SW, Suite 300
Calgary, AB T3E 6L1

Editors: Lexie Angelo
Cover Design: Lexie Angelo

ISBN-13: 978-1-990201-14-1

Printed in the United States

For Mackenzie

Contents

The Assistant

I came early and found my spot. A dense copse of cedars to the southeast of her grave, about fifty meters out. Or were they pine trees—I don't know. I keep my distance. Sticking to the guilt complex I've always had. Watching behind a tree with my cheek pressed against its bark like the criminal they think I am. It's coarse on my skin and I breathe through my nose to hide the fog from my breath. Smells of forest meld with November rain as it falls and then dribbles down the side of my face. My teeth chatter, mostly nerves. An umbrella would've been nice, too conspicuous though.

Under an awning a small crowd gathers in chairs around her plot. Did her only surviving son show up? It is too far to match any of the faces to my memory of his framed picture. I knew she didn't have much family left, just the son, in his late sixties. And I'm keeping my distance so there're no questions. They're grieving after all, I shouldn't hassle them. But I have to be here—for her—I couldn't miss it. And like I said, I don't want any questions.

They're lowering her down now. With those belts and hydraulic lifts that grind and shutter, the machinery of death. Or post-death I guess—they didn't kill her.

I whisper, "I'll see you on the other side, Hildy."

The gleaming black casket sinks into the bowels of the earth. Or at least it's small intestine. Six feet under with all her secrets, she descends an inch at a time.

Maybe it's what she deserves.

Can't take all her secrets.

I've got one.

The one.

It's complicated, of course. I'd never killed anyone before. And I don't plan on repeating it. Besides, if I'm the only one who knows, what choice do I have?

And how else would you hear about it?

It all started in late July when I saw her peeking through her window. It was the second time I had delivered a package to her. The third time, I waved and saw her half-moon face behind those thick Art Nouveau blinds. She thrust them closed as our eyes connected. Like she had something to hide. I didn't get a good look. It's not like she couldn't see the big delivery van with that fake fuckin' smile dashed across the side.

Don't worry, I intimate sidling up their walk, *I'm only here to drop off your order, promise this is no home invasion.* And then I smile. Sometimes I wave to the little camera in the doorbell, the middle classes' one defense against people like me—a delivery person.

I'm too tired at the end of each shift to pick up a book, let alone write a sentence. That part of me atrophied a long time ago. I was going through the motions by that point. Primed for someone, anyone.

But she hid her face so quickly, like a little kid scared when I returned her looks. How was I supposed to know she'd mean so much?

Those were the first few times. On the fourth or fifth delivery, she'd opened the door. It was early August by now.

"Mornin'," I beamed, as the door cracked open six inches. The safety lock was still in position. I lifted the package. "Just a delivery."

Her eyes narrowed. "What's your name?"

I rested my foot on the first step of her porch. "I'm Ted." I don't know why I lied but it felt right. Maybe 'cause my first instinct was she'd complain about something, they usually do. "And what's yours?"

She gave me a suspicious look and then motioned to the package in my hands.

"Ah, sorry, that should've been obvious." I checked the address. "*Hilda*, how you doin' today? That's a nice name."

She smiled, somewhat forced and then unlatched the safety lock to open the door a few more inches. "Are you the young man that's been delivering my packages?"

I leaned on my bent knee, nodding. "Yup, that's me, this is my route." I motioned to the houses around her block. "I deliver to everybody in the neighborhood."

Her lips parted, a real smile this time. Like something clicked.

I handed her the box. "Have a nice day."

That was the first time I talked to her. But not the last and if I'd known what she'd ask of me I'd have turned around, asked for a new route. Now it's too late. Here I am, watching them stand and say goodbye for the last time before throwing their flowers on her casket to decay and then forget her. It's in the earth, now, can't see her. And the rain stopped, it'd been more a drizzle. Or *miasma*, as Hildy might've said.

I'm still here to make sure they treat her right.

We talked about death, her and I, she told me it's nothing to worry over. She must've sensed my anxiety.

"*After* death," she said, "will be the same as *before* birth." That was Schopenhauer. I figured it out later. She wouldn't tell me who it was.

But the sight of dirt and earth thrown on top is too much. It constricts my throat, as if they're sprinkling it over *my* casket. What if it sifts through the seams? Sometimes I make myself fantasize about my own funeral, and then the decomposition. When the maggots and worms slither in and out of my eye sockets and then slip into my gaping mouth. That's where I'm headed.

A man who might be her son, stands at the edge of the grave mumbling into the void and then scatters a fist full of damp soil.

I have to look away. My van's parked in a lot to the south. I should head back 'cause I still got deliveries. The only thing of value I create.

After that first visit a few packages passed without contact—and then one day she was waiting with the door open, no safety lock this time, in her robe. The sun was out and it kissed the top of her head as she leaned for support on the door. Her white patchy hair glowed in the warm light like a lambent halo. She was in a purple-fleeced robe. Somehow it made her face seem longer, more sallow. There was a sag in her bottom lip. She waved as I ambled up the stairs, and kept hold of the doorframe.

"Just in time," she said with a smile. "I need help arranging some chairs in the back." She let go of the doorframe to wave behind her. "Too heavy at my age."

"Yeah, no problem," I said, "I got a few minutes, I can help."

I didn't have extra time but something spurred me on. Like she'd been waiting for me. It was nice to be needed.

Her arm was soft and warm, comforting, as she looped it through mine for support and then half-led, half-followed me around back. We passed through two side gates, a vent billowing the scent of Tide fabric softener, and then into a fenced-in backyard of brick tiles. Two square mats of AstroTurf were centered on her patio butted-up against a deck.

"Used to be my dog's washroom," she said. And that's when I realized she had an accent. The hard W in 'wash-' came out as a soft V, a linguistic fingerprint. As if she'd pared it back, lobbed off the doubled U for a single V. That faded sound was what drew me in, what hinted at more than just an old lady.

I cocked my head to the side. "Where're you from—originally?"

 "Germany," she said dismissively, and then pointed to a few cast iron chairs around a table with an umbrella. "Could you move them counter clockwise? Match the angle of the sun?"

After, we stood on her deck and talked. She told me about the passing of her husband, Heinz.

"About 22 years now."

She hobbled to her sliding glass door to reach inside for something.

"Let me show you a picture."

I admired as best I could the faded print of the couple from the sixties, judging by her green with white polka-dotted blouse and his blue corduroy jacket. Their faces were out of focus.

"I can't even drive without him," she said

I handed back the picture. "Never got your license?"

Staring at the image she waved her other hand. "Of course I have, got it a long time ago." And then she asked about me. "Are you in school—is this a summer job?"

14

"No, not anymore. Mom got sick," I said. "Had to dropout to work, that's why I'm slavin' for Amazon. It's just the two of us and we need the money."

She interrupted, "Studying what?"

I looked down, and replied, "Literature."

I caught a gleam in her eye. Turns out she was a retired English teacher. Well, there ya' go. Small fuckin' world. She grinned when I said that I was a big reader and dreamed of writing fiction.

Before I could ask whom she read she changed topics so quickly it gave me whiplash.

"What do you think of the new deck?" she said.

I glanced around, shrugged. "Looks great."

"They did a wonderful job." She pointed out the treated wood. "Such a lovely shade of maroon, don't you think?" And then she told me about the guys who put it in last summer. "Some other workin' men," she said with that soft V. "Please, wait here, I have something for you."

I took a seat on her deck in a big red folding chair, glad for the break from work. I'd take the cool breeze of Hildy's backyard over lurching through traffic any day.

She came back with a little bundle of something wrapped in tinfoil. "Banana bread," she said. "Payment for helping."

I munched on it for the rest of my deliveries. Couldn't get her out of my head.

It was only a few days later that I had another package. As I pulled up, I wondered what she kept ordering. Before I started up the path, her door was open and she stood leaning on a polished black cane, smiling. Her face seemed to age over the few days since I'd seen her. She looked gaunt. Hunched. And there was a distance behind her eyes.

But I grinned as I skipped up. "More chairs?"

"No chairs," she said. "But I was thinking of moving my birdbath around." Arm-in-shaky-arm we shuffled to the back. We stood there almost twenty minutes before she asked if I'd be interested in having a look.

"Come down and peruse," is how she phrased it. I told her I didn't have much time. I was on a schedule and all that.

She arched her brows. "Well, at least let me wrap your banana bread." By that time I'd given up trying to be efficient—I'd do anything to get out of that fucking cesspool-of-traffic. I liked gabbin' with Hildy and despite our age we clicked with an old familiarity that's hard to describe. There was depth below her calm surface. Like a sneaker wave she sucked me in and then dragged me out to sea.

And I let her.

The next delivery was no different. She had her purple robe tucked around her as I strolled up. The way she stood could've been in some old silent movie staring, Frau Hilda Heinrich. That was her last name, Heinrich. She always had a package. Shit, she always had *had* a package.

It was theatrical is all I'm saying. The way she closed her robe. Wrapped it around herself in such a slow way, I had the feeling she wanted me to see how her purple slip with that floral print motif matched her lipstick. It wasn't scandalous—she was just trying to look nice. She must have been a little shaky putting it on, the lipstick;

she'd gone outside the lines. It would of been comical if there'd been intention. Sometimes it's hard to keep inside the lines though, I know that.

I'd barely handed her the package before she asked,

"What are you reading?"

That's what she had wanted to show me last time.

"Come have a look at Heinz's collection."

Climbing her steps I remembered what she had said about Heinz. That he was her knight in shining armor, a moralizer, so to speak. He did everything for her, and that's what made it so hard after his passing. She didn't even know how to balance a chequebook.

It was a hot August day when I stepped inside her little bungalow. The blinds were open and sun poured through her large bay windows.

"Ah, the AC is so nice. It's frosty in here."

"I like it that way," she said. "Keeps the wrinkles down." Followed by a little wink. And that's what I mean—she was sharp for her age.

"I never read them anymore," she said, as I followed her through the living room, past the mustard-yellow sofa encapsulated in a clear plastic covering. Which, I fucking knew would be there, that plastic covering, I mean. "And since Heinz," she said. "They're just collecting dust."

She tottered through her home pointing out pictures of her kids on the wall, one living—a son, the others dead. She'd outlived two of her children.

"My son may as well be dead," she said. "For the amount he sees me."

Other framed pictures ranged from the early sixties to the late nineties—original mounted pieces of artwork. Some were expected, one of a glossy bowl of fruit, another of an empty rocking chair in front of an old hearth. Kitschy grandma-type shit. Others were darker. She was a connoisseur of abstract expressionism. The one that stuck with me was a painting of a set of mal-formed teeth, just the teeth, grotesque and crooked and gaping on a black background, in smears of peach and stark white, gnashing out in pain. In rage.

"I moved everything to the basement a few years ago." She paused at a set of stairs leading down through a doorway. "They kept reminding me of him, his ideas, his passions. His histories. They're all too much, but if you're interested—"

"I mean, sure, ya. I'd love to have a look, thanks."

"My hip can't make the trip down, I'm afraid," she said. "I haven't been in ages, and you're warned: there will be dust."

She explained that the books on the left wall would all be in the original German, but the right was in translation, as original as they could be. Heinz had wanted to assimilate, so once they'd emigrated, everything they read was in English.

The basement was a room of forgotten passions. Old desks, cabinets, and exercise equipment from the previous century shoved in the corners, sure, but more, much more—an entire universe. From above, like wide-set weary-eyes squinting through cataracts, two foggy pot lights illuminated the space. I made out shelves on either wall, each lined with leather-bound spines, tomes of a dark tone. Snooping through her space gave me a thrill like peeking in the medicine cabinet while in someone's bathroom.

The air was stale and thick but as I neared that complex earthy scent of mold from the pages was sweet. Intoxicating like stacks in an old library. I started in the German section and checked the titles I pulled at random. Had to be Heinz's philosophy shelf. I couldn't read them but recognized names. I pulled Kant, Hegel, Schopenhauer, Nietzsche, and Heidegger.

I couldn't believe it. Hiding underneath this old lady were three centuries worth of German Idealism. I knew the original copies would be worth some money, so I skipped to the translations.

My mouth dropped as I scanned the shelves. Heinz *was* a reader. Spine after spine my eyes widened. Not just German. The complete works of Dickens, Dostoyevsky, and Defoe. Hugo, Flaubert, Proust. An original Spanish Don Quixote next to a translation.

I had a stack of fifteen books wedged in my arms. All hardcover. But, I still had deliveries to make. Before heading up I checked for an original Kafka. My old Lit professor would've killed for an original, *Die Verwandlung*, and I'd dreamed of reading it in the original. Maybe Hildy could've coached me through. But most of the shelves I couldn't inspect. Next time.

Little did I know the next time was the last I'd see Hildy alive.

As I summited the stairs her grin showed off her yellowed and translucent teeth.

"Are you sure you don't mind me borrowin' these?" I glanced at the excess of books cradled in my arms. "Some of these gotta be worth money..."

She waved away my pretense and then topped off the stack with a foil wrapped slice of banana bread. "Ted, they're yours now. No use to me." She took my arm in both of hers and then led me to the front door. "And how pleased Heinz would be, to have a young reader value his collection. You may even come across some of his notes or marginalia, to have a little conversation with my Heinz."

Once I finished work for the day, I went home to page through my new additions. I dropped the stack on my particleboard coffee table and excitement filled me. There's no substitute for Kafka, but Mann's not bad, and I had snagged *A death in Venice*. No one writes surrealist novellas like the German Modernists. I leafed through it as I sprawled on my sofa with earplugs in to block out the live punk music pouring in from across the street.

Once I skimmed over Von Aschenbach's debauchery I knew Hildy was an asset. Raised on her mother tongue and an English teacher she would of had the insights, known the subtleties that translations can't confer—even the better ones.

I told myself if she didn't have another package soon, I'd stop by on my own to check-up on her.

I spent the rest of the evening in Heidegger's *Being in Time*, and a couple Nietzsche texts. Hildy was right. I found a slew of annotations. But there was a second, finer hand with slimmer looping L's that seemed feminine. In Nietzsche there were underlining's of questionable passages. About the *Übermencsh*, I noticed, and *The Will to Power*. The concepts that got N. in trouble. Some odd lines with aggressive talk about "The Jews" jumped out at me. N.'s worst takes seemed to be Heinz's favorite.

Was the plot thickening?

Or thinning—maybe—I'm not sure.

It's pouring rain now, and I leave the cemetery before they run for their cars. It is easier this way. I got what I came for. Hildy didn't strike me as someone worried about closure. What closure I have is in those books. I still have one last delivery for her. I've been saving it for after the funeral. It must have been on backlog or something. It's a thirty-five minute drive to her neighborhood.

I had been dyin' to ask her about Heinz's reading. What was the purpose of such a close analysis of these couple texts? None of the others had as many notes or the second handwriting. I'd imagined sitting around her living room with stacks of books spilling at our feet discussing Nietzsche's inherent contradictions.

The door was open when I sauntered up. She had on the same purple robe, the same long flowing purple slip. Except now her lips were red, and she topped off the outfit with a sun hat, straw and tan. I should've taken this as an omen, the red lipstick, but I was too wrapped up in German phenomenology to consider this pagan portent.

"I was just wonderin'," I said, bouncing down her walk, excited to talk obscure theory. "When I was gonna have another delivery for my *literary patron*."

I paused with her package under my arm and my foot on the usual step. Trying to amuse. I liked when she laughed. "How you feelin' today, Hilda? You look nice. I like the red."

She looked down. A malaise seemed to set in. Unaffected, she wasn't playing coy to my compliment. Despite her age she always had quickness to her, a spark. But that was gone. She was weary.

"Please, come sit with me." She held her robe closed with a balled fist. She reached for me with a shaky hand so I hurried up the steps to support and then escorted her to the sofa. At that point I would've carried her if I had to.

It was mid–afternoon, early September by this time, but still hot. The sun spilled on my back at that little spot on the neck where the hairline ends but before the shirt begins. That little amount of skin exposed there, as I stepped into her stagnant air that skin on the back of my neck that was getting a minor sunburn went clammy and prickled. The blinds were closed and there was a low thrum of the outdated air conditioning unit shoved in one corner next to a cabinet with glass doors displaying stacks of unused, undusted ceramics. My eyes adjusted. It was the same living room as before, but something had settled.

"I have something I need to say, *have* to say, I think you're the one to...to..." Once we reached the sofa she touched the armrest as an anchor and then turned to wave me to sit. "What did you think of Heinz's library?"

I wanted to ask about Nietzsche and all the notes, but something was off. I told myself it was the cold as my teeth chattered and the skin on the back of my legs stuck to the plastic covering. She had 'em on the goddamn loveseat, too. Still hoping to chat literature I shrugged it off as she lowered herself an inch at a time until the last six when she let herself drop like dead weight.

She winced while adjusting. "Please, tell me though, what did you read?"

I shifted around trying to get comfortable. "You were right, Heinz *was* a close reader and note taker." I looked down, thinking about the annotations I'd studied over the last few days. The odd and definitely problematic passages I re-read with intention like I was putting together a puzzle. "Yeah," I said, glancing around the living room. "Grabbed mostly philosophy, read some Heidegger, Nietzsche, some really interesting stuff I wanted to ask you about." As our eyes connected there was that spark. "It kinda looked like there were *two* different sets of handwriting?"

She smirked with a playful scoff, a second flicker, like I'd picked up the trail she'd laid for me.

"That could be."

She crossed her ankles out in front of her and then smoothed down the creases of her robe. "But all of those notes are from before. From our old life, the old us. But that's why you're here, I need your help."

She shot another look at me. "We have a story, Heinz and I."

"What old life? Before you guys moved to The States?"

She nodded with reserve.

"You mean in Germany?"

She flinched. A silence had settled. I waited.

"In Germany," she said at length. "During the war."

"*Okay*," I drawled. "During what war? You don't mean, like, *The* War, do you?"

She swayed with acknowledgment. I kept quiet. Something was building in her, begging to get out.

"Alright," I said. "So like, did you guys have to run from the Nazis or something?"

She covered her face, and then let out a wail of sadness I'd never heard. She shook.

As I watched her contort, all the stories about survivors ran through my head. Was Hildy some long-lost cousin of Anne Frank? I reached to comfort her and told her it was okay. She covered her face. "Of course it was horrible for you," I said. "To see your country and people swept up in the madness."

"You don't understand," she cried through her hands. "It wasn't them that was evil—"

She stopped to uncover her face and look up at me. "It was us."

I stayed with Hildy that afternoon. As she talked, all the notes I had read connected. She said she was born in Berlin in 1932. And then became the teen bride to one of Joseph Goebbels' cabinet members in '45. He wasn't that old at the time; Heinz was twenty-seven when he married her at thirteen. He'd been a promising philosophy lecturer at the university of Frankfurt (post-Adorno, et al.—I had asked). Actually worked under Heidegger, if you can believe that. But when the Nazi's had been at their strongest, Heinz got recruited to the propaganda campaign. They had used the German intelligentsia to brainwash the public and rationalize their massacre. Heinz's intellectual labour had been used to control and manipulate. But the worst part, she had said, was that *she* had also been an aspiring philosopher. A true wunderkind. She had started reading the Classics at age six, and had worked on a dissertation by twelve. It was her *and* Heinz that had cherry-picked from the German theorists.

It was this little old lady's scholarship that had helped collate and then propagate the justification for the German ethnocentrism. It was her, she had said, who first prompted Heinz to propose the idea to Goebbels of the Übermencsh or *Overman* as being a German, an Aryan superman. It'd all just been so theoretical, she had said.

And then it wasn't.

She then told me about the weeks spent in The Bunker, during the last few days of chaos and mayhem but before the cyanide capsules. Heinz had organized an escape with his underaged bride. They had landed on Ellis Island in '47. She had got her license in the '50s. I asked why she was telling me this.

"I can't leave with these secrets," she said. "Someone had to know."

I stared at her. Unsure of where I came in. I tried to imagine a thirteen-year-old Hildy in a Nazi uniform, saluting. It tasted bitter.

"I want you to write my story. I'll pay you, and then you have to do one last thing."

Well, I needed the money. Obviously. I'd been pissing in plastic bottles for the last six months to increase my earnings. No time for a fuckin' bathroom break when you're paid on commission. The dark shit is what happened next. I said I understood why she had to tell someone, and that her life could make a great story, but why me?"

"I could have gotten another, well-known-writer to tell my story, but I need you, I can tell you're the one. And there's that last thing." She stared into the china cabinet, absent. But what could she tell? That I was desperate, broke, or that I'd keep her secret and not call the Israeli defense force? Or was there something else?

Once she snapped out of her reverie she cut a cold side-glance at me. Staring into my eyes she said, "I have stage four colorectal cancer, and it's aggressive."

She wouldn't see the doctor anymore. But knew she couldn't die before telling her story. *Cleansing my soul*, she kept repeating. And she needed help. She didn't want to be here anymore with all the pain. After her darkest secret was out.

"I can't go on, but I can't *go* either," she whispered. "*The Will to Life* is too strong, the *survival instinct*. I can't swallow the pills, I've *tried*."

All the packages I had delivered were chemicals, pharmacology. Pancuronium bromide, potassium chloride, and a dose of midazolam for sedation—the same cocktail used by the US government to execute their people. Which was appropriate, that America would provide the efficient means of death to a Nazi, one more time.

"I can't do it myself," she said. "I need your help, and this, here—"

She reached under her pillow and said, "This is for you."

It was a blank envelope with a bit weight to it.

"Twenty five thousand," she said, studying my face. "All you have to do is mix this powder—" she pulled a little glass vile from her robe pocket "—into my tea, or dinner, anything, just don't tell me, I can't know, otherwise it won't work!"

She thrust the vile towards me.

"I've written out a last statement so there'll be no proof you were ever here."

"I can't fuckin' do this," I said. "You're fuckin' crazy." I tossed the envelope on the corner of her bed and walked out.

I've been a lot of things in my life, but never a murderer. Not even the assistant.

There's something about driving through the rain. Windshield wipers shedding water off glass like clockwork. Lights glow. Yellow, red, green, and then I start out. With this next turn I'll be in her neighborhood. I've got her package pulled out. It's sitting on the passenger seat next to the books. I've kept them around to help remind me of her. Of the complexity that is a human life, and a long one at that.

I don't regret what I did. Or what I didn't do more like. I left her house that day and haven't seen her alive since. That's why I went to her funeral to say my goodbyes. I don't miss leaving the money, either. But what I do lament is leaving another human in pain. She begged for help. Said she couldn't take the guilt and shame or pain anymore. And I left her there. After she swore off the doctor, I knew it would be torture. I left her to suffer.

Freud took lethal doses of morphine in 1939 after battling mouth cancer. He was eighty-three and chased out of his beloved Vienna by the Reich—he didn't have much left either. Why was my moral outrage so strong when confronted with a morally stronger case? Wouldn't I have gone back in time and killed Hitler? By leaving her there in distress, suffering—didn't *I* kill her?

I pull to a stop in front of her bungalow. A huge tree in front towers over her front yard. Killing the grass. I grab her package with scuffed corners.

One last package she'll never open.

What the fuck is it?

It doesn't sound like much when I shake it. When I inspect it again I see something new. The sender information is the same as the delivery.

From/to:

Hilda Heinrich

1724 Lepscene Drive

Boise, Idaho

And the return to sender label looks homemade. But instead of sender, it says Ted.

My mouth drops. And the sinking in my stomach in a split second swells to my throat. It's for me.

Opening someone's package is a federal offence. But it's got my name on it. Well, not *my real name* per se, but Ted, nonetheless. Should I open it?

It's kind of like the golden rule for delivery drivers: Never open the package.

But it says Ted. And that's all Hildy knew.

I slice the bottom corner with my apartment key and then peek inside. There's an envelope with that bulge and a bit of weight to it. But that's not all. There's another slip of paper, folded. It's a hand written note from Hildy, to me.

Dear Ted,

For all of my life I have had that cruel secret. Since I was a girl, from thirteen I have been split in two. Please understand, there had to be a second, stronger me to deal with those months in the Reich. Wading through those brief, temporal nights of such despair that followed made me fear for the Eternal Night. My secrets slept well in the underworld, but their geist never could. The darkness engendered in me from repressing what we did and to whom we did it to, has finally seen light. I never understood the hateful ideation, yet I went along with it, I was no better. After that despicable treaty of Versailles my family had nothing, Germany had nothing, and the resentment grew. We ate potatoes until the Studienrat noticed my marks in gymnasium. You must believe me, it was the only way to pull us out of the gutter and make Father proud. It felt like a utopia at first, but once the vague daydreams of racial hygiene that had fringed the edges were no longer vague, it was too late. The banality of the evil was what allowed it to creep in. I watched the most brilliant minds of the university fall for the same promises and ignore the same signs.

When I met Heinz, everything changed, I loved him. No matter what he dragged me into it would always be the two us. He promised my family would be safe. And they were, until the Soviet tanks crushed their bones in the spring. I lost everything. The shame has eaten away at me, maybe that is where the cancer came from, from my secrets.

Heinz said, we did the best we could with what we had, but no one knows what it was like unless they were there. You would have been one, too, Ted.

I know it is not much I am leaving you but I have decided it is yours, after what I put you through. Perhaps it will be enough to quit your job and write our story. Do not be angry with me, there has been that worm at my core for all these years. We all have it, that worm, the knowledge of inevitable death, only, I could see yours more clearly. But they are different. Ours are different. Finally though, I can breathe. Thank you, Ted, for listening.

Please, forgive me, and yourself. We are not guilty anymore.

Love,

Hilda Heinrich

I fold the letter and slip it back into the box with the sealed envelope.

She's right about the worm. I've known it's there, slithering around. But that it is different from hers—I'm not so sure.

She knew what she did. Had over seventy years to think about it. Not once did she make the effort to share, to absolve or ask forgiveness, until it was too late. That's all she had to do, tell someone. But she was a child at the time. And couldn't. She had to harbor it, shove it down, deep to the core. Where she couldn't get to.

That's the one thing I won't do. Harbor it, bury it.

I put the van in drive and then head home. I'm done.

ACKNOWLEDGEMENTS

Special thanks to Michelle Spencer for wading through my earliest attempts at meaning making. This story would not be here without her. Thanks to the Alexandra Writers' Centre, specifically Robin van Eck and Cindy. Big thanks to everyone at Short Story Salon for sitting through my long, over caffeinated readings. Thanks to Lori D., for being a close reader and friend. Special thanks to my parents, Doug and Janell Schabell, for being my first readers and conversation companions.

ABOUT THE AUTHOR

Josef Schabell is an emerging author born and raised in the Northwest United States. He half-heartedly attended school in North Idaho where he studied psychology and philosophy. He is a member of the Alexandra Writers' Centre and is currently working on a short story collection and a novella. He lives and writes in Calgary, Alberta with his wife, Mackenzie, and cat, Cat. He may be reached at jascabell@gmail.com

SPECIAL THANKS

Calgary Arts Development

Calgary Public Library

IngramSpark